DOWN INTO
THE
NETHER

AN UNOFFICIAL OVERWORLD ADVENTURE, BOOK FOUR

DOWN INTO THE NETHER

DANICA DAVIDSON

Sky Pony Press
New York

Copyright © 2016 by Danica Davidson

All rights reserved. No part of this book may be reproduced in any manner without the express written consent of the publisher, except in the case of brief excerpts in critical reviews or articles. All inquiries should be addressed to Sky Pony Press, 307 West 36th Street, 11th Floor, New York, NY 10018.

Sky Pony Press books may be purchased in bulk at special discounts for sales promotion, corporate gifts, fund-raising, or educational purposes. Special editions can also be created to specifications. For details, contact the Special Sales Department, Sky Pony Press, 307 West 36th Street, 11th Floor, New York, NY 10018 or info@skyhorsepublishing.com.

Sky Pony® is a registered trademark of Skyhorse Publishing, Inc.®, a Delaware corporation.

Visit our website at www.skyponypress.com.

Minecraft® is a registered trademark of Notch Development AB. The Minecraft game is copyright © Mojang AB.

10 9 8 7 6 5 4 3 2 1

Library of Congress Cataloging-in-Publication Data is available on file.

Cover design by Brian Peterson
Cover artwork by Lordwhitebear

Print ISBN: 978-1-5107-1220-1
Ebook ISBN: 978-1-5107-1221-8

Printed in Canada

DOWN INTO THE NETHER

CHAPTER 1

WE HAD TO HURRY, OR ELSE THE MONSTERS would get us.

There were five of us kids running across the Overworld, trying to get to safety before the sunset. As soon as it got dark, monsters—better known as mobs—would spawn and search for their prey.

"Do you think we can make it to the portal before dark?" cried my best friend Maison.

With any other portal in the Overworld, we could just stop and build it. But this was a special portal we were going to, because it was the only one that led us to Maison's world, Earth.

"If we hurry," I said, hoping I was right.

Yancy and Destiny, who were beside us, were also from Maison's world. The last person in our group was my cousin, Alex. Alex, like me, had been born and raised in the Overworld, and she'd only recently learned that other worlds existed.

1

It hardly seemed real, but just last night the five of us had all worked together to fight Herobrine. Everyone in the Overworld knew about Herobrine, though they thought he was just an old ghost story for kids. We knew better. Nightmares about Herobrine and music discs with prophecies had taught me that Herobrine was real and that all he wanted was to ruin lives and destroy worlds.

When we fought Herobrine at his temple lair on top of a mountain, he disappeared. Did he disappear because we had defeated him, or was he hiding and would come back to attack us later? That's what we didn't know. And because of that, we were terrified!

At least I got Ossie back, I thought, pulling my cat close. Herobrine had stolen her, the way he stole other people's most prized possessions, and we'd saved her on the mountaintop.

"There's the portal!" I said.

The last rays of light were creeping down the horizon as we caught sight of the house the special portal was kept in. I pushed open the door and we all crammed into the little house. The portal sat right before us, glowing red, green, and blue in the middle.

"Phew," Yancy said, huffing and puffing. He put his hands on his knees. "After all that fighting and traveling, I am going to sleep well tonight."

"We can rest tonight, but we need to get back together tomorrow," Alex said, in her usual take-charge manner. "If Herobrine is still out there, we have to plan and be ready for him."

"Do you want to come to our world with us?" Destiny asked, concerned. "It might be safer there."

It was a nice offer, but there was no way Alex and I could go to the other world right then. We needed to get back to my home and try to find my dad, because he'd been brainwashed by Herobrine. He had falsely believed that my friends and I were the ones causing all the damage that Herobrine actually caused. Like the other people in the Overworld, Dad had suddenly turned mean and suspicious, because that's how Herobrine changed people. If Herobrine was really defeated, hopefully Dad would be okay now.

Alex grinned and shifted the bow and arrows she had on her shoulder. "Oh, don't worry about Stevie and me," she said. "I know it's getting dark out, but I'm not scared of any mobs."

I didn't feel as confident as Alex at all. I looked down at the diamond sword I held in my hand. I'd only recently started to get good at fighting mobs, and I still made plenty of mistakes.

"Then just be extra careful," Destiny said, and gave Alex and me a quick hug good-bye.

Maison took my hand in hers and looked at me with a serious expression. "It's going to be okay, Stevie," she said. "I'm sure your dad will be waiting for you back at the house and he's just fine. And if Herobrine is still out there, you know we'll find a way to take care of him. We're your friends, and we'll get through this together."

I took a look at the others around me. A few months ago, I never would have guessed that I, Stevie, an average eleven-year-old boy in the Overworld, would find a portal to a new world and make all these new friends. There was Maison, who was smart and brave and my best friend, even though we were from different worlds. There was Destiny, who was a little shy sometimes, but who always tried to do the right thing. There was Alex, who loved adventure as much as the next person loved a good mushroom stew, and who I was finally getting to really know. And there was Yancy, who . . . who . . .

"Toodles," Yancy said in a singsong voice, waving his weird fingers at us. I still had a hard time taking fingers seriously, even though all the people in the other world had them. I still thought that fingers looked like little squid tentacles attached to hands.

"Yeah, see you," I said, not very enthusiastically. I still felt uneasy about Yancy.

He was the whole reason Herobrine existed.

Yancy used to be what you'd call a "cyberbully." Because Maison's computer acted as a portal to the Overworld, he'd hacked her computer and tried to have a zombie takeover. His cousin Destiny helped Maison and me stop him in the end, and afterward he went into therapy and said he was a new, better person now. Which I had a hard time believing.

Back in his cyberbullying days, he had put a mod of Herobrine into the game. That mod gained consciousness and became the Herobrine we were fighting. Yancy kept pointing out he'd just put Herobrine in the game as a joke, and he hadn't meant for Herobrine to gain consciousness and become an evil monster bent on destruction.

But there was another reason why I was scared of Yancy.

Remember those music discs that told prophecies about Herobrine?

One of those prophecies said that Herobrine wouldn't be easy to defeat. That he'd keep coming back.

Another of those prophecies said that the five of us were destined to fight him. However, the music discs also warned that one of us would betray the rest and put our whole mission in jeopardy. And I knew in my heart I could trust Maison, Alex, and Destiny.

I didn't know if I could trust Yancy.

CHAPTER 2

A s ALEX AND I WATCHED, THE REST OF THE group jumped through the portal, vanishing to the other side. I felt a ton of relief knowing that Maison and Destiny were safe now, plus I was glad to have Yancy out of my hair. He was seventeen, and sometimes he tried to act like we should listen to everything he said because he was the oldest person in our group. So at worst he was a traitor and at best I thought he was still pretty annoying.

One deed was done, but there was still something else pressing on me. "Now let's get home so I can check on my dad," I said.

Alex nodded in agreement and creaked open the door, letting us peer out. The Overworld landscape had turned dark with freshly spawned zombies and skeletons skulking. In the light of the square moon I could see that the skeletons were all holding arrows.

"Oooh," Alex said. She looked so determined she might as well have been rubbing her hands together. "This looks like a challenge."

Would it be terrible to admit I was eleven years old but I still didn't like the dark?

"I'm ready," I said, because I didn't want Alex to think I was a big baby.

The two of us charged out into the night, Ossie beside us. We headed for my house. We didn't go out of our way to attack mobs, but if any crossed our path and attacked us, I hit back at them with my diamond sword and Alex got them with her arrows. And let's just say a lot of them crossed our paths.

"Is it true that in Maison's world there are no zombies or hostile skeletons?" Alex asked, drawing back her bowstring and hitting a skeleton.

"Yeah," I said, thinking people in Maison's world were super lucky because they didn't have to deal with this every night. A zombie lurched up on me from the side, moaning, its green skin rotten and smelling bad. My cat Ossie jumped on it with a hiss, her claws out, and I stabbed the zombie with my sword. Just like that, the zombie was gone.

More zombies came moaning and appearing out of the shadows, but they were far enough away that Alex, Ossie, and I ran ahead instead of attacking them.

"Look out!" I said. A skeleton appeared overhead, arrow at the ready, aiming for me. My first thought was to duck out of the way, but before I could move, Alex's arrow hit the skeleton straight on. The skeleton jolted. Alex hit it again and the skeleton was gone as if it'd never been there to begin with.

"Thanks, Alex," I said.

"No problem," she said. "I get lots of practice slaying mobs when I go exploring—Zombie!"

I hit the zombie to my left. I'd been able to hear that zombie's moaning from way off. I was just waiting for it to get into my reach.

When my home came into sight, Ossie's ears drew back and she began to hiss. Something was moving around the house. *A lot* of something.

"No," Alex whispered, stopping beside me. "It can't be. . . ."

In the shadows by the torch lights, I could see a swarm of zombies and skeletons all standing around the house as if they were guarding something. The torches brought out the moon-white bones of the skeletons and the deep green of the zombies. I could see a white sign propped against the door that said, DID YOU THINK YOU COULD DEFEAT ME THAT EASILY?

CHAPTER 3

WHAT DO WE DO?" I YELPED. I DIDN'T KNOW what was panicking me more right then: the mocking sign that Herobrine had obviously left, proving he was still alive, or the fact we probably wouldn't be able to even make it to the house. There was no way the two of us could take out this many mobs!

"You take zombies, I'll take skeletons!" Alex called out as a group of zombies lurched toward me. I was lifting my diamond sword in a flash, hitting back at all of them. The skeletons didn't bother coming close to us, because all they had to do was raise their bows and in seconds we were being rained on by arrows. I had to dodge the arrows while Alex took the skeletons out.

Then I thought of something really obvious.

"Dad!" I shouted, hoping he'd come bursting out of the house and help us. Dad was the best mob fighter around, and he'd bulldoze through these mobs. There was no way Herobrine could have brainwashed Dad so much he wouldn't help his own son survive a mob attack.

Alex heard me shouting, and she began to shout for him, too. "Uncle Steve!" she yelled. "Stevie and I need your help!"

But Dad didn't open the door. It was as if he wasn't even home.

No way! I thought. Dad always stayed indoors when it got dark out. Even if he couldn't hear Alex and me shouting, he had to be able to hear all the zombies and skeletons.

"Run!" Alex yelled. I looked over and saw she'd taken out all the skeletons that had guarded the door. That opened up a lot of space, though we still had to get around the zombies. There was still a ways to go before we'd make it to the door.

I stabbed at a zombie and then dove forward. Another zombie swiped at me, knocking me off my feet. I hit the ground, groaning on impact. Zombies jumped over me, only to find themselves quickly full of Alex's arrows. Alex leapt beside me and grabbed my hand. Zombies staggered just behind our feet, moaning. We ran as quickly as possible.

"Stevie!" Alex cried, shoving me forward. A zombie struck her. She didn't fall down, but she crashed into me, which sent me tumbling and almost losing my grip on the sword. With zombies swiping at us, we slashed and hit back until we reached the house. I hit the button to open the door and Alex, Ossie, and I dashed in, the zombies at our heels.

I used my sword to knock back all the zombies trying to rush in. *Come on, come on!* I silently yelled at the door.

The door finally shut, closing us off from the mobs.

Outside we could hear the zombies crying out and scratching against the house, trying to find a way to get in. Dad had built the house solidly, but their deep moans and scratches lurked behind the door.

Alex and I collapsed on the wooden floor. We were both badly hurt. I called out again for Dad. My voice just echoed in the empty house. He definitely wasn't here.

Alex saw the panicked look on my face and said quickly, "It's okay, Stevie. He's probably out looking for you. We need to get something to eat now so we can feel better."

"But Herobrine is still out there somewhere," I said, turning to Alex, my eyes wide. "You saw that sign in front of the house. No one other than Herobrine would leave that."

"It could be someone else playing a cruel joke," Alex said. I could tell she knew this explanation was a stretch. Herobrine had left us cruel, taunting signs like that before.

We dragged ourselves into the kitchen for food and milk. It would bring back our strength. I also gave Ossie some fish. As we ate, we felt our health improve, and then I started to feel a little less panicky. Alex was probably right—Dad was out looking for me, and he was just fine. My dad was famous in this area for being the best mob fighter around, which earned him the nickname "The Steve." Someone as famous as Dad should be safe outdoors at night. I hoped.

"Those mobs . . . might have been a little more than a challenge," Alex said as we began to feel better. I could tell she was embarrassed that we hadn't been able to take all the mobs out.

"My dad says, 'Sometimes your only option isn't a pleasant one.'" Unfortunately, that got me thinking about my dad again. And I began to worry.

Alex and I both ended up sleeping in my bedroom because it made us feel safer. Ossie curled up at the foot of the bed and lay down, purring. After being in Herobrine's clutches, she must have been extra happy to be home.

Before lying down, I sat on the edge of the bed, holding one of the music discs. The musical discs usually talk all the time, saying prophecies that only the five of us—Alex, Maison, Destiny, Yancy, and me—could hear. But now the disc was silent. I kept staring at the disc and holding it, willing it to give us some clue of where Dad was.

Nothing. All I could hear was the moan of zombies just outside our door.

I fell asleep almost immediately after lying down, still all sore and aching from the zombie attack. And then I started to dream.

In the dream Maison and I were both in her world. We were building stuff with logs from her fireplace and having a good time. It felt like when Maison and I had first met. Back then I didn't really have any friends in the Overworld, and kids at Maison's school had been bullying her something terrible. So when we first became friends, it felt like we didn't have anyone else in the world. I felt so lucky I had found that strange portal and discovered Maison's world and Maison.

In the dream, Maison said she was hungry and so we both peered inside her refrigerator, which is where people in her world kept all their food. Maison had introduced me to all sorts of things they ate there, like cheeseburgers and cinnamon toast and grilled cheese sandwiches.

I knew exactly how Dad and I harvested or made all of our food, but that wasn't the case for a lot of people in Maison's world. As far as Maison was concerned, food magically appeared after her mom used little green things called money to buy the food from the store.

There was a package in the fridge that was reddish but also had some white in it. The color reminded me of the shade of rocks found in the Nether called Netherrack. I'd only been to the Nether a few times with Dad, but that underground, fiery world sure did leave a scary impression on me. It definitely wasn't a place I'd go to for fun.

"Whoa, you have food made from Netherrack?" I said, impressed.

Maison rolled her eyes, though she was smiling. Sometimes our worlds were so different we got cultural things all mixed up. "That's raw beef, Stevie," she said. "That's the stuff we use to make cheeseburgers. The color just looks similar."

We started to laugh at the confusion.

"But how does this become cheeseburgers?" I asked. "Do you use a crafting table?"

She started to tell me something about a stove, and then suddenly stopped and became very quiet.

The room felt as if the temperature had plummeted. And I could feel a presence with us. An evil presence.

"No," Maison said, sensing it too.

Suddenly Herobrine loomed overhead. His eyes had no pupils and he stared at us from the deep depths of those white pools. None of the ghost stories I'd heard as a kid prepared me for how spooky it was to look into those cruel, vacant eyes.

Maison was frozen beside me. When I tried to draw my diamond sword, I realized I was frozen, too.

"Good evening, Stevie," Herobrine said, in a voice that was so harsh and so soft at the same time. A whisper dripping with poison.

"Herobrine!" I said. "We beat you on the mountaintop!"

Herobrine laughed as if I'd told a good joke. "Oh, I disappeared, but I wasn't defeated. You know my story, Stevie. Yancy created me as a joke, but then I started to become aware of my surroundings. Because I was originally built from Yancy's anger, I fed on the anger of the world, and it became my mission to bring more anger. Haven't you noticed how the people around you have grown so angry and suspicious of one another lately? That's my doing, and I'm only getting started."

"You put the mobs in front of my house, didn't you?" I demanded. "You're the one who left that sign?"

Herobrine smiled wickedly. "Guilty as charged."

"Well, we got past your mobs," I said, seething. "We're safe from them now."

"Your father did do a good job at making that house mob-protected," Herobrine said. He grinned wider and leaned in on me, his eyes gleaming in their happy madness. "But that's okay. I don't want your house. I want something better."

Something better? I swallowed, and then I realized.

"The portal," Herobrine whispered, knowing exactly what I was thinking. "I want the portal to your friends' world."

"No!" I said, struggling harder than ever to draw my diamond sword. It was useless; I still couldn't move. What had Herobrine done to keep us from moving? "You can't go through that portal."

"That's why I'm so interested in you," Herobrine went on as if I hadn't said anything. "You're the boy with the portal. With that portal I can go into your little friend Maison's world. And do you know what I'm going to do there?"

"Stop it!" I shouted.

"I'm going to take it over," he said. "I'm going to turn people against one another. That will be the start of my powers. But my powers will keep growing, and the people there will be helpless to stop me. They think *Minecraft* is just a game, and most of them out there won't even recognize me. Isn't that a grand plan, Stevie? I want you to say 'good-bye' to your good friend Maison right now, because you'll *never* see her again."

CHAPTER 4

COULD MOVE AGAIN! I LASHED OUT AT HEROBRINE, but this woke me up and I realized I was fighting with the bed covers. Sunlight filled my bedroom and the zombies were all gone from outside the house. Ossie was still with me, and I could hear Alex downstairs, muttering something to herself.

Dad still wasn't home.

I quickly got dressed in a turquoise shirt and purple pants. When I got downstairs, I saw Alex had already dressed in a green shirt and brown pants and had fed herself breakfast. She was gathering her toolkit and bows and arrows.

"Oh, hey, Stevie," she said when she saw me. "I wanted to let you sleep in so you'd be all healed up. How are you feeling?"

There was a storm going on in my head. I couldn't figure out what to do. In my heart, there was a terrible aching. I looked at her and said mechanically, "I slept okay."

I couldn't tell her what I'd dreamed. And I definitely couldn't tell her what I had to do. I was scared she'd try to talk me out of it.

"I'm going to the village to ask about your dad and see what's going on," Alex continued. "I'm bringing along one of the music discs just in case it starts giving prophecies again. You eat breakfast, and when I get back we'll go to the portal to see Maison and the others. Okay?"

I didn't want to tell Alex that this wouldn't be possible. I couldn't lie to her, either, though. "Mmm," I said, all noncommittal, because that could mean anything.

Once Alex was out the door, I ate a quick breakfast for strength. Everything tasted like sadness. I picked up one of the music discs again, and shook it in anger and desperation.

"Please!" I begged. "Give me a clue! Don't make me have to do this!"

The music disc was silent. I threw it across the room and put my head in my hands. I didn't want to not have Maison in my life.

But if I didn't do anything, Herobrine might . . . he might. . . .

I couldn't let myself think of what he might do to Maison or her world. I found myself picking up Dad's diamond pickaxe without thinking and putting it in my toolkit. I picked the music disc back up, still hoping it might say something. Ossie followed me outside and we walked through the sunlight, past flowers and oak trees.

I noticed that none of the trees I passed had any leaves. That gave me a shudder. Leaves falling off trees was a sign that Herobrine was nearby.

I went to the house that held the portal and slowly opened the door. Once I stepped inside I could only stand there, heart pounding in my ears.

I put my hand against the side of the portal. Maison had first made this very portal when she was playing *Minecraft* on her computer, back before she knew *Minecraft* was a real world. She's found weird stones she'd never seen before—I'd never seen any stones like them either, to be honest—and tried her hand at making something new. That was how this special portal came to be, though none of us could have predicted just how it would work!

Ossie mewed up at me. I could tell from her eyes that she knew something was wrong.

Slowly I reached into my toolkit and pulled out the diamond pickaxe.

"I'm sorry, Maison," I said. I only knew one way to prevent Herobrine from going through the portal and destroying Maison's world. I would have to destroy the portal first.

When the diamond pickaxe hit into the stone of the portal, Ossie cried out as if she were trying to stop me. She jumped on my shoulder, mewing and clawing at me.

"No, Ossie!" I didn't realize how close I was to crying until I heard it in my voice. I forced Ossie off my shoulder and she gracefully landed on the floor, staring up at me with hurt eyes. As if I didn't feel terrible enough already.

"I'm sorry, Maison," I said again, hefting the pickaxe. No matter how many times I apologized, it wasn't going to feel like enough. I hit the portal. Again. Again. The stone blocks split noisily and broke into pieces. The portal collapsed down all around me, demolished.

When there was nothing left to save, I let the diamond pickaxe fall to the ground.

I stumbled back home, head down, feeling shaky. I imagined that after a good night's sleep Maison would wake up and head to her computer, ready to go through the portal and check on how I was doing. However, her computer screen would be solid, like all the other computer screens in her world.

"Stevie!" I imagined her crying out when she couldn't get through. She would hit the computer screen with her hand and then pound on it with her fists.

Maybe she'd think it was just a sad mistake. She'd probably never guess that I was the reason our two worlds would never see each other again.

"I hope you understand why I had to do this, Maison," I found myself whispering to her again, as if she could hear me. What I wouldn't do to hear Maison's voice one last time!

When I walked back over the hill and got a glimpse of my house, I saw two things. The first thing was Alex running as fast as she could over toward the house, a scroll rolled up in her hand. The second thing I saw was a new white sign propped up against the house. I knew it was a message from Herobrine, but I was too far away to read it.

"Stevie!" Alex exclaimed when she saw me. Changing directions, she dashed my way, out of breath by the time she reached me.

"Did you find out anything about my dad?" I asked immediately, even though I didn't want to hear her answer. I could tell from her face that whatever she'd learned at the village, it was bad. Really bad.

"No," Alex gasped, shaking her head. "I couldn't even get into the village. There are guards everywhere, and people fighting, and . . . and. . . ."

Trembling, she slowly unrolled the scroll.

"I found this on a tree not far from the village," she said.

On the scroll there were drawings of Yancy, Destiny, Maison, Alex, and me. Underneath, it said: WANTED. ARREST ON SIGHT.

CHAPTER 5

I SNATCHED THE SCROLL FROM HER. "PEOPLE WANT to *arrest* us?"

She nodded. "It must be because we helped Yancy escape from the dungeon."

When we'd brought Yancy back into the Overworld to help us fight Herobrine, Yancy had quickly been arrested. And we'd had no choice but to break him out of the dungeon. It had been extra weird because the guards who arrested him worked for Mayor Alexandra, who was my aunt and Alex's mom. Now we were all criminals. Aunt Alexandra was another one of the people who'd been brainwashed by Herobrine.

"We have to go through the portal and find the others," Alex said, hefting the quiver on her shoulder. "We'll tell them about the sign from last night, all the zombies and skeletons waiting for us. . . ."

"Um, Alex," I said slowly.

"Maybe they'll have clues on their end, too," Alex went on, already making purposeful strides toward where the portal used to be.

I fidgeted. "Alex," I said again.

Alex stopped and glared at me in frustration. "What, Stevie?" she demanded. "It's not like we have time to spare!"

I stared at the scroll in my hand. It wasn't very long ago I'd been a hero because I'd saved the Overworld from a zombie takeover, and now I was one of the Overworld's most wanted fugitives. And somehow all that was still less painful than telling Alex the truth.

"What is it, Stevie?" Alex said, stomping close to me. Fear replaced her usual take-charge persona.

"We-can't-go-to-the-portal," I said. The words were so mumbled and strung together I could barely even understand them myself.

"Huh?" Alex asked.

"We can't go to the portal," I said more carefully.

"Why in the Overworld not?"

"We can't go to the portal because. . . ." Stop. Deep breath. "Because the portal has been destroyed."

"No!" Alex cried. "Can it be rebuilt?"

I shook my head. "No, it can't be rebuilt."

"That rotten Herobrine!" she raged. "He must have done this!"

She was really making this difficult. "It wasn't Herobrine," I said.

She turned wide eyes on me. "Then you know who did it? Tell me!"

I was trying really hard to stall and think of a way to tell her the truth. Except I couldn't think of a non-terrible way to say it, and my guilt felt hotter than the lava of the Nether. "Well, you see, I know it wasn't Herobrine because. . . ."

"Because?" she prompted.

There was no non-terrible way to say it. "Because I was the one who destroyed it."

Alex grabbed me by my shirt so forcefully I thought she might knock me over. "You fool!" she roared. "What were you thinking?"

I tried to wrestle out of her grip. "I'm having a hard enough time with this myself!" I wailed. She released my shirt with disgust.

"It makes no sense that you would destroy the portal!" she ranted, storming around in circles. "You will never see your best friend again. You know this, right?"

"I know, I know!" I said. "But what was I supposed to do? Herobrine showed up in my dream last night, saying he wanted me because I was the boy with the portal and that he was going to destroy Maison's world. What was I supposed to do? I had to save Maison and her world! I tore the portal to pieces so Herobrine has no way of getting there."

Alex still looked disgusted, but now at least she seemed to understand a little, and that made her stop yelling and storming around. "Why didn't you tell me about this dream and your plans?" she asked.

"Because I was scared you'd talk me out of it," I said. "It's the same reason I didn't go through the portal one last time to say 'good-bye' to Maison. If I got talked out of it and then Herobrine destroyed their world, I'd never be able to live with myself. It's like my dad said, sometimes you have to do unpleasant things because you don't have any other options."

At this point I was sniffing and sniveling and I could tell Alex didn't know what to do with me. She sighed and put her hand to her forehead, thinking long and hard.

"Okay," she said. "Okay, we'll have to figure out something else now. If there are wanted posters for us, it won't be much longer before people come looking around here to take us to the dungeon. You do realize that, too, right, Stevie?"

I sank down on the ground and Ossie rubbed against me, trying to give some comfort. No luck. "It never ends, does it?" I said. "My dad's missing, Herobrine is still on the loose, we're going to be caught and put in a dungeon. And all I can think about right now is how much I want to hear Maison's voice again."

That's when I heard Maison call out, "Stevie! Stevie, where are you?"

CHAPTER 6

ALEX AND I BOTH WHIRLED AROUND, AND FOR one heart-pounding moment I thought I would turn and see Maison there, safe and sound and still able to visit the Overworld. But the fields around us were completely empty.

"Stevie!" Maison called again, sounding more panicked.

Alex and I both looked down. The music disc I'd brought with me was spinning and glowing.

"Maison!" I cried, putting the music disc close to my face.

"Stevie, is that you?" Maison asked frantically. Her voice was definitely coming from the music disc. "I don't understand this. I hear you, but I don't see you."

"I can hear your voice on a music disc," I said.

Maison gasped excitedly, understanding. "Me, too!" she said. "Yancy forgot to take the other music disc out of his backpack when we got back, and I have it here in my bedroom. It's spinning and glowing and I can hear your voice."

"Yes, yes!" I said. "I can hear you, too!"

Alex's eyes bulged. "Amazing!" she said. "Those music discs are working like . . . what are those things they have in their world that let them talk to each other no matter where they are?"

"Phones!" I said. "They're working like phones. Oh, Maison, I never thought I'd be able to talk to you again!"

"Stevie, I tried to go through my computer portal when I got up this morning," Maison's voice came out. "Except it's not letting me through. I invited Destiny and Yancy over, and they can't figure it out, either."

I heard Yancy's voice then, as if he were standing behind Maison and leaned in to get closer to the music disc.

"Yo, Stevie!" he said. "Do you have any idea what might be preventing us from getting through the portal? Because we, like, *really, really, really* need to talk with you."

Alex leaned in and answered for me. "We need to talk with you, too. The portal's gone."

From the music disc I could hear Maison, Yancy, and Destiny all exclaiming in shock.

"No way, no way," Yancy said.

"That can't be!" Maison said.

I hung my head, feeling the heat in my cheeks, too embarrassed and ashamed to explain.

"That's not all," Alex said. "When Stevie and I got back to his place last night, Herobrine had surrounded it with mobs and left a sign out front. Stevie's dad is missing, and when I went to look for him in the village, I learned that all five of us are wanted for arrest. And then Stevie had a dream about Herobrine last night that said he was going to destroy your world . . ."

"But why is the portal gone?" Destiny asked. "We need that portal, right now!"

Alex gave me a do-you-want-to-explain? look. I didn't want to explain so I turned my face away.

"Stevie destroyed the portal," Alex said. "Because he wanted to protect you from Herobrine."

"Oh, Stevie, say it isn't so," Yancy said.

"It's true," I said. "I didn't want to say anything because it hurts so much, but this means that even though Alex and I still have to fight Herobrine, you're all safe from him."

There was a long and terrible silence. At first I thought the music disc was broken, but then Destiny said in a frail voice, "Should we tell him?"

Yancy cleared his throat. "Stevie," he said. "Herobrine tricked you. I know you meant well by destroying the portal, but that's really the worst thing you could have done. You see, Herobrine is already in our world."

CHAPTER 7

"**N**o!" I stammered. "No, that can't be possible! I broke the portal, so there's no way he—"
Yancy cut in then. "He got out through the portal last night, Stevie, before you destroyed it. All destroying the portal did was trap him here in our world."

"Are you sure?" Alex demanded.

"I had another Herobrine dream last night," Yancy said. "He was mocking me, saying he'd faked us out at the temple so we'd believe he was gone. But all he did was jump into the *Minecraft* game on my phone and we carried him through the portal and into our world without even knowing it."

I remembered how Yancy kept his *Minecraft* game on his cell phone, and how we'd played the zombie noises on it to distract the guards so we could break Yancy out of the dungeon. At the time the cell phone had seemed like a miracle worker, but now this!

"It's worse," Maison said. "When I turned my computer on this morning, there was Herobrine's face staring back at me from the screen. He said, 'I am Herobrine, and you will all be receiving a visit from me shortly. Your world is doomed.' I ran to my mom, and her computer was doing the same thing!"

"You don't mean—" Alex began.

"He has taken over all the computers, phones, and tablets in the world," Destiny exclaimed. "Everyone with one of those devices saw him and heard his message."

"It didn't matter where they lived or what language they spoke," Maison said. "He spoke the same message in different languages. He wants everyone to know he plans to destroy our world."

"But that's so arrogant, and that will be his downfall," Alex said. "If he's told all the people in your world that he's going to attack, then you can all band together."

"The news is reporting that Herobrine's message is part of some virus or prank that took over everyone's devices," Maison said. "They're trying to blame different groups and governments. No one is going to believe us when we tell them who's really behind it. Everyone else thinks *Minecraft* is just a game."

"Has he done anything else besides sending the message to everyone?" Alex asked.

"No more messages since the one this morning, but he's definitely letting his presence be known," Yancy said. "People are coming home to find their houses ransacked and their possessions stolen. Crime is up. People are scared and angry."

"Was there anything else he said on the message this morning?" Alex wanted to know.

There was another long silence. "Yes," Yancy said finally. "He said, 'It won't be much longer before my armies and I advance on you. And when your world is destroyed, you can thank Stevie for me.'"

CHAPTER 8

THAT'S WHEN I ABOUT LOST IT. "No!" I CRIED, covering the sides of my face with my hands. "No, this can't be! I destroyed the portal to protect you!"

Overcome with horror, I turned and ran from Alex. She shouted out to me and I ignored her, racing all the way to the house. Herobrine's sign remained propped out front, taunting me. When I got close enough to read the words, I let out a choked cry.

STEVIE, YOU ARE THE TRAITOR FROM THE PROPHECIES.

"No!" I cried. "No!"

Alex ran up behind me, holding the music disc close. I saw her eyes scan over the sign, reading it. "I—I don't understand," she said, suddenly not so take-charge anymore.

I whirled on her. "Of course you do! I betrayed everyone because I trapped Herobrine in their world!

He can do whatever he wants with them now. I'm the terrible traitor the prophecies all talked about! It was me all along!"

By yelling like that, I was taking out my anger and horror on her, even though she didn't have anything to do with the choices I'd made. I'd been the one who destroyed the portal without discussing it with any-body else. I had destroyed it because I was so certain it was the only thing I could do to save the others. *Me, me, me*, a whole world was about to be destroyed because of me!

I could hear Yancy talking through the music-disc phone, asking Alex what was going on. In a shaky voice, she told him what the sign said.

Maison's voice got on the music-disc. "Stevie, don't believe it!" she said. "Herobrine is just calling you the traitor to upset you. That's what he does!"

"But he's right!" I said. "All this time, I was so sure Yancy was going to betray us. I . . . I never thought . . . I was really trying to help. . . ." I trailed off pathetically. There was nothing more to say.

"Stevie!" Yancy said. "Listen to me, man. Maison's right. You can't beat yourself up over this. All you have to do is make a new portal and we can all get together again."

Alex seemed to brighten up at this idea, but I knew it wasn't that easy.

"I can't remake the portal," I said. "When Maison made it, she used stones she'd never seen before. I'd never seen those stones before either, so how would I know where to find them?"

"Yancy, you made a new portal," Maison said, "when you hacked my computer. Make a new one now!"

I heard clanking noises, which I guessed were computer keys. Then I heard everyone on the other side gasp.

"What is it?" Alex demanded. I stared intensely at the music disc as if it would let me see what was going on over there.

For an answer, we heard Herobrine's voice.

CHAPTER 9

"**T**HERE'S NO NEED TO BE ALARMED," HEROBRINE purred evilly.

"He's on my computer screen again!" Maison exclaimed. Alex and I hushed, not wanting Herobrine to know we were listening in.

"Oh, I'm on more than your screen," Herobrine said. "I'm everywhere now. Were you impressed this morning when I spoke to people in all different languages? That was nothing. When I hacked everyone's system, I not only learned their language of choice, I learned a lot of unpleasant and embarrassing things about them that I'm all too ready to share with the world. Thanks to me, everyone's personal fears and embarrassments will become common knowledge as I spread it throughout the Internet. That's another form of what you call cyberbullying, right?"

"You're lying," Yancy said. "No one is powerful enough to hack everyone."

"Yancy, oh, Yancy," Herobrine said. "I enjoyed hacking your email. Teenagers do like to write angsty, diary-like stuff, don't they? I found out that you'd been emailing some pretty private, personal things to your therapist. It's very good reading. Remember that time you were in fifth grade and all the kids egged you and chased you home after school?"

"You had no right to read that!" Yancy yelled. "That's just for my therapist and me!"

"Seems you were bullied pretty badly before you decided to act like a bully yourself," Herobrine said. "That's often how it goes, though, isn't it? Bullies make bullies. You made me."

"I didn't know kids did that to you," Destiny said in a hushed, shocked tone.

"It was because he was too smart," Herobrine mocked. "So good at math and science and computers, so bad at being sociable. Apparently in your world that's a bad thing! The other students were envious of his good grades and took it out on him. He used to come home crying almost every night in elementary school and would hide his cuts and bruises from his parents. He felt like the most helpless person in the world, until he discovered he could bully online, where it didn't matter if he wasn't sociable or wasn't strong enough to beat up others. It was the perfect platform for him to take his anger out on the world."

"I'm not like that anymore," Yancy said through gritted teeth.

"It doesn't matter," Herobrine said. "I took every negative and embarrassing piece of personal writing of yours and published it online. Now the whole world knows. Look!"

"No!" Yancy said.

Alex and I stared at each other, alarmed. We couldn't see what was happening, but we had a feeling Herobrine was showing the websites that held Yancy's darkest and most private secrets.

"I have to take those things down!" Yancy said, and I heard the clanking of more keys.

"It's gone 'viral,' as you like to say," Herobrine said. "Millions of people must be reading it by now. Just think of this as your reward for betraying me at the temple. And speaking of traitors. . . ."

Herobrine's voice sounded as if he were grinning. "Stevie!" he called. "I can't see you, but I know you're listening in."

What should I do? I thought. *Try to pretend I wasn't listening? Speak up and confront him?*

Before I could figure out what to do, Herobrine went on, "Stevie, thank you so much for aiding and abetting me in my takeover of Earth. I couldn't have done it without you and that portal! I especially love that this happens after you've been acting so self-righteous and so suspicious of Yancy."

"I don't know what you're talking about," Maison said. "Stevie isn't here, and he can't hear you." I knew she was trying to protect me.

Herobrine chuckled. "I find that highly unlikely," he replied. "But if you're telling the truth, I have a message for you to pass on to our dear old Stevie. Tell him as much as I enjoyed kidnapping his cat, it's no skin off my back that Ossie is safe with him again. Tell Stevie I captured a much bigger prize this time."

It was then the last piece of the puzzle fell together. "Dad!" I cried out.

CHAPTER 10

"**S**TEVIE, YOU ARE LISTENING!" HEROBRINE gushed. "Yes, Stevie, it turns out that your father might be the most feared mob slayer around, but capturing him was easy. He's here on Earth with me, and you can come see the two of us the next time you go through the portal."

He stopped and laughed. "Oh, that's right—you destroyed the portal and can never return to Earth again. Well, I'll have to say 'good-bye' to your dad for you, since you were never able to."

"Don't hurt my dad!" I shouted. "Give him back to us! Herobrine! Herobrine!"

But there were no more words from him.

Yancy exclaimed, "The computer crashed!" And then there was chaos on the other end.

"What crashed into them?" Alex asked worriedly. She didn't understand the slang from the other world. "Are they hurt?"

Destiny got on the music-disc-phone. "Herobrine disappeared from the screen and then the whole computer stopped working. Yancy's trying to turn it back on."

Several tense minutes passed. I'd never felt more useless in my life.

"It's not working!" Yancy said. "I'm calling tech support."

Maison got on the music-disc-phone then. "Oh, Stevie!" she said. "Are you okay?"

I was panting and trying not to be sick. Alex saw I was in no state to talk and quickly replied for me, "He'll be fine. What about you?"

I heard Yancy in the background, yelling, "What do you mean, you can't help us? Guys, tech support is saying that *everyone's* computers just crashed and they're swamped!"

"Everyone's computers?" Destiny breathed. "Then there's no way we can make a new portal here."

Overwhelmed, I grabbed the music disc right out of Alex's hands. "Maison, Maison!" I called. "I'm so sorry! Please, you've got to help my dad!"

"We'll do everything we can, Stevie," Maison said. "But this is a big world and Herobrine could be anywhere. And without any computers to do research on where he is—"

Yancy spoke to me then, serious and straightforward. "Stevie," he said, saying my name like a general says an order. "It's up to you. You and Alex have to find a way to make a new portal to our world. It's our only hope now."

Alex looked deep in thought, her hand to her face. I was mad at my helplessness and the fact that Yancy thought I could do something about building a new portal.

"Don't you get it?" I shrieked. "I can't make a new portal! I don't know where to find those stones. I've never seen stones like that before or since, and neither has my dad, and he knows everything there is to know about the Overworld."

Alex came out of her thoughts slowly and spoke, "I've seen those stones before."

I turned to look at her. "You have? Where?"

"A long time ago," she said. "I came across those stones during one of my trips to the Nether."

"The Nether!" Maison said. "That's it! You and Alex have to journey down into the Nether and find those stones again!"

"It's not that easy," Alex said. "It's not like I have a map, and the Nether is always dark. That means there are hostile mobs no matter what time of day it is. Even if we find the stones, there's no guarantee we'll find our way back, or even make it back without being overrun by mobs."

"So you can't do it?" Destiny asked.

For the first time in a long time, Alex smiled. "Oh, I never said that," she said. "I'm always up for a good challenge."

"Then hurry!" Maison said. "Time is running out!"

CHAPTER 11

ALEX GRABBED ME BY THE SHIRT AND YANKED ME over to the shed where Dad kept all his supplies. My dad was a big believer in preparedness, so his shed was chock-full of useful things he'd collected over the years.

"Alex, what are you doing?" I asked, stunned.

She was already hauling out Dad's supply of obsidian. "I'm making a portal to the Nether. What does it look like?"

"I—but—do you even remember where you saw those stones in the Nether?" I asked.

I could tell the others had already made up their minds that we had to go to the Nether, and it was our only option. But the Nether was so unsafe. This underground world was dark and crammed with lava and monsters, and you could only get to it—or get out of it—through special portals. I'd barely ever been to the Nether, and the only time I had gone was with Dad. I wasn't allowed to go without an adult. I'd done things like stop a zombie takeover of the Overworld, but Dad still said that going into the Nether by myself was out of my league.

It was incredibly easy to get lost and not find your way back to the portal. We could be trapped there forever. Cliffs jutted out over fiery depths and lakes of lava. Half-broken bridges gave people the impression they could cross from one rock to the next . . . only for them to fall down, down, down below and never be seen again.

And then there were the mobs. Go into the Nether, and you might find yourself face-to-face with a ghast, a white flying creature with a box body and tentacles. It looked kind of like a squid, only it could fly and it would hurl fireballs at you. And water changed to steam in the Nether, so if you got hit by the fire, you were out of luck.

Unfortunately, ghasts were only the beginning. There were also blazes, which were little fiery yellow mobs that could burn with fire without getting hurt. They could hurl *three* fireballs at a time. Magma cubes looked like little square heads that hopped around, which might be pretty funny until they transformed into multiple smaller magma cubes and all attacked you. And don't forget the wither skeletons. These were kind of like the skeletons we had in the Overworld, but they were striped black and carried vicious-looking swords.

There was still the Wither, a giant mob boss with three heads that could fly, spinning over you while it attacked. It shot blue skulls at you, and those things were so dangerous they could destroy something as solid as obsidian.

Normally if you got hurt you needed food and rest. That was basically impossible in the Nether. If you made a bed to rest, that bed would just explode on you. Even beds here were dangerous.

In other words, take whatever is bad and scary about the Overworld at night, multiply it by like ten times, and then you have the Nether. Plus eternal darkness. Plus lava everywhere. There were endless reasons why I was scared of the Nether.

For some reason, none of this seemed to be bothering Alex. "No, I don't remember where exactly I saw those stones," she said matter-of-factly.

"So we're just going to go traipsing around the Nether, which is a totally enormous territory, and just hope we stumble across the stones in time to stop Herobrine?" I asked, annoyed. It sounded ridiculous! "Besides, even if we find those stones, who knows if it'll even work to make a new portal? Maybe Maison has to make it from her computer and it can't be built on our end. It's not like we've ever made one of those portals before!"

Alex was in the middle of stacking the obsidian blocks together to make the portal, and now she turned and glared at me, hands on hips. "I know it's crazy," she said. "But the point is: can you think of anything less crazy?"

"Yes!" I said. "*Anything* else!"

Alex stepped up and got into my face. "I don't think you understand the situation, Stevie," she said.

"At least this is doing something. How else are we going to save your friends *and your dad* unless we find a way back to their world?"

Bringing up Dad was an especially low blow, because there was no way I could argue with that. And I couldn't come up with any other better ideas. I started to stammer nonsense and Alex said, "All right then."

She went back to putting the portal together while I hovered anxiously over her. First she put the black obsidian blocks in a frame shape, making sure there was enough space in the very middle for us to get through. For the last bit, Alex got out some flint and steel to make the fire in the middle. That's what made the portal come alive. The center of the portal burned bright purple with more purple flakes trembling in the fog. It sure was a pretty portal for something that would take you to such a nasty place.

I called into the music disc, "Maison, can you think of any other ways we can get back to your world? Has Yancy fixed the computer yet?"

There was a moment of silence. I didn't think anything of it until there was another moment of silence, and then another. I shook the music disc.

"MAISON!" I shouted at the top of my lungs. When there was still no response from Maison, my stomach plummeted to my feet.

Alex snatched the music disc from me. "Is it broken?" she asked, shaking it as well.

I had a much worse first thought: *What if the silence meant Herobrine had already gotten them?*

A strain of music came out of nowhere. For a moment I thought it was from the music disc in Alex's hands, but then I realized it was coming from her toolkit. Alex snatched the toolkit up and pulled out the third music disc we'd found. The music disc we'd used as a phone was as silent as could be, but this music disc was spinning without a jukebox and releasing those music notes.

Alex and I stared at each other over the music disc, hopeful and startled and daring to believe. Was it going to be another prophecy?

The music creaked out, spooky and dark and sinister like the Nether. Then a harsh voice began to speak, the words lined up almost as if they were poetry.

"The king of mobs has escaped the Overworld.
He eyes the prize of another world.
The stones for a new portal
call out from their home in the Nether.
A traitor by mistake can be a
hero by his actions.
It is only by confronting the darkness
that Herobrine can finally be defeated."

That's when the music disc began to glow. One long stripe of light flashed out from it, pointing to the Nether portal—pointing to our destiny and the destiny of the two worlds.

CHAPTER 12

"**D**O YOU THINK IT WILL LEAD US TO THE STONES?" I asked in a whisper. I could barely say the idea out loud because it was so explosive.

Alex shook her head, and I swore I saw a little smile. "I've never heard of music discs doing that," she said. "But I've never heard of them working as prophecies, either. I say we follow this disc and see where it leads us."

I knew then that there was no more time for fighting the idea of going down into the Nether.

Alex packed up more weapons and supplies and the two of us approached the Nether portal, her first. I still held my music disc close to me, hoping against hope I'd hear Maison's voice again.

Ossie rubbed against my legs, taking me out of my thoughts. "Oh no!" I said. "What do we do with Ossie?"

Normally I would have felt fine leaving Ossie in the house by herself. That was in my pre-Herobrine life. I

47

didn't want to tempt fate by leaving her unwatched and taking any chance of letting her get snatched again. However, I also didn't want to bring her into the dangers of the Nether.

Ossie started rubbing against the portal as if she approved of it. That silly cat.

"Well, I guess she made up her mind on her own," Alex said. "Why don't you carry her on your shoulder so she doesn't wander off?"

Good thinking. I lifted Ossie up and set her securely on my shoulder. "You stay close, Ossie," I said, and she rubbed my head and purred as if agreeing.

"I'll go first," Alex said, and leapt through the portal and into Nether.

I waited, took a deep breath, and then jumped through after her.

For a moment everything went purple and hazy. Then I fell through and into the Nether, falling clumsily on my hands. "Ouch!" I said, because Ossie's claws dug into my shoulder so she could hold on. As strange as Maison's world was to me, especially when I first saw it, I can't say it was as alien to me as the Nether.

The air was dark red, as if you mixed together the colors of night and spider eyes. Above us we could see the ground, giving me a closed-in feeling. How could anyone live without seeing the sky or sunlight? The stones around us were all reddish and built into random plateaus and jutting edges. Here and there were blocks of flames, their orange-red fires licking up as if to taste anyone who might fall on them. The darkness went on and on and on, enfolding us.

And we were not alone.

Just a few feet away were a whole herd of zombie pigmen. They had bodies shaped like the bodies of zombies in the Overworld, but their skins were blotched with both zombie green and pig pink. They even had little pink pig snouts, and I remember Dad telling me they couldn't be hurt by lava, and that you can create a zombie pigman by having lightning strike a pig. Not that I wanted to create any more of these things.

I saw the golden swords they were carrying, and my hand automatically raised my diamond sword in defense.

"Stevie, no!" Alex cried, thinking I was going to attack them. "Zombie pigmen leave you alone unless you hurt them, and then they'll start defending themselves. Viciously. And trust me, you do not want that whole swarm on us."

"Right, right, I knew that," I said. And I had known that—Dad had drilled a million rules about the Nether into my head over the years—but I was so worried about Dad and everything else that it had slipped my mind.

"Ah ha!" Alex said, noticing that the glow on the music disc she held was pointing us eastward. Or, at least, I think it was east. It was really hard to tell directions in this underground world.

Alex briskly began walking the way the music disc wanted her to go, strolling right by the zombie pigmen as if they didn't bother her in the least. I nervously followed, staring at the zombie pigmen, expecting them to get us.

When the portal was far enough behind us that it was almost out of sight, Alex stopped and pulled some supplies out of her toolkit.

"What are you doing?" I asked, confused, my eyes darting around for any signs of danger. There were several more swarms of zombie pigmen I could see, but no overly dangerous mobs. The zombie pigmen grunted as we walked by.

"If this music disc stops working—or, if it leads us in the wrong direction—I'm not getting caught looking like an idiot," Alex said. "My mom taught me that when you're in the Nether, you always leave yourself a trail so you can follow your way back out."

I was glad that Alex was thinking through these things. I knelt down and helped her set up a torch on the ground by putting a stick and piece of coal together. Within seconds the torch was working just fine, a little fire among all the other fires here.

"Stevie," Alex said as we started walking again, "I can tell you're super nervous, but it's okay. These music discs haven't lied to us before, and we should be able to get the stones and make the new portal in no time. Once we get the portal made, we join with the others and make more plans. If you try to figure out everything now, it'll be too much."

I guess she really did think it could be that easy. "It's too much already!" I said. "What if we don't even make it to the stones because we're attacked by mobs? The Nether is a dangerous place, Alex! It's not some fun adventure."

"If you have an attitude like that, life will be miserable," Alex said. She suddenly stopped and looked at me straight on. "Wait, I get it," she said. "You're scared of the Nether."

"I'm not scared!" I said, even though I knew everything about me said otherwise. I was basically shaking there, looking left and right and clutching my diamond sword.

"I know your dad told you that sometimes you have to do unpleasant things," Alex said, "but it's also true you can make things unpleasant just by expecting them to be. Look, even your cat is more excited about this Nether adventure than you."

Ossie purred and rubbed against my head. Darn cat.

We came up to a bridge between two cliffs of rock. Peering down, we saw a lava lake below. Even from up here I could feel its heat against my face. I didn't want to think about how much it would hurt to touch it. Or to fall into it.

The bridge shook unsteadily as Alex and I made our way across it.

"At least it's a full bridge," Alex said, since bridges in the Nether often broke off into nothing and didn't actually get you anywhere. "I still think this music disc isn't going to take us anyplace bad."

She spoke too soon. When we stepped off the bridge and onto the other cliff, we heard an awful sound coming our way. It sounded like a baby crying, or someone having a really hard time breathing. Soft and creepy at the same time. Before we could even think of how to respond, three ghasts burst out of the darkness, coming straight for us.

"Duck!" I cried as the ghasts opened their mouths and hurled balls of fire.

CHAPTER 13

ALEX AND I BOTH DOVE TO THE SIDE, NARROWLY missing the fireballs. I felt the heat of one fireball whiz by my face and go over the cliff, landing in the lava below. In the panic Ossic jumped off my shoulder and ran.

There was no time to call her back. Another fireball blasted at me, and it would have hit my shoulder if I didn't roll away as fast as I could. Alex was jumping and rolling, too. She kept trying to shoot with her arrows, but the fireballs came at us so fast she wasn't getting time to aim. And whenever a fireball hit the ground, it exploded and turned to flames.

In a rush I got back to my feet and lifted my sword. I knew it was possible to use weapons to hit the flames back at ghasts. If you hit them back with their own blast, that was a good way to defeat them. Too bad I'd never had any practice doing it. A ghast blasted at me and I swung and missed.

Out of the corner of my eye I saw Alex, still ducking and blocking, trying desperately to get a shot in. Another fireball shot out at me and I swung, missing again. One ghast was especially interested in getting me, and the other two circled over Alex, spraying her with flames. The ground below us chipped away as more fires leapt up from the fireballs.

I swung my diamond sword, and this time I felt the impact as my sword struck the fireball. Finally! But then I saw the fireball shoot back toward the ghast and just barely miss it. So close!

The ghast overhead zipped around, making me turn toward it with my diamond sword out. I realized it was trying to push me closer toward the edge of the cliff.

"Alex, help!" I called out.

"I could use some backup myself!" Alex cried. She aimed her arrow at one of the ghasts. The other ghast opened its mouth to blow fire at her, but she jumped away from the fire blast just in the nick of time.

I could tell that the ghasts were trying to push Alex over to the cliff as well. They weren't just trying to take us out with their spitting flames or knock us into the fire they created—they wanted us to fall into the lava pit below, where there was zero chance of survival.

"Alex, we have to stay on the cliff!" I said.

"You think I don't know that?" Alex snapped back.

Ossie came running back out of the red-blackness and threw herself on one of the ghasts circling over Alex. She landed on top of the white square head and dug in her sharp claws. This startled the ghast, who began swinging in circles, trying to knock Ossie off.

Now that Ossie had the second ghast busy, Alex jumped up, ripped back her bow and sent an arrow flying, taking out the other ghast over her head. As soon as her arrow hit the ghast, it disappeared into nothingness.

"Good job, Ossie!" I shouted. Big mistake. Hearing her name, Ossie looked up for a moment, and the ghast was able to knock her off its back. Ossie landed on the red rocks just beneath her. Thankfully she was not hurt. Alex drew back her bow and took out the ghast Ossie had been attacking.

The ghast over me continued to press in, shooting another round of fire. When I swung my sword, I felt the blade hit fire again. This time the fire shot back and struck the ghast straight on, making it vanish.

"Yes!" I said, feeling victorious. Stevie: one. Ghast: zero! *Maybe I shouldn't be so scared after all*, I thought.

"Stevie, look out!" Alex yelled.

I almost didn't see it before it was too late.

The moment before Alex's arrow hit the third and final ghast, that ghast had let out one last breath of fire. The fire was hurtling my way!

I dived to the side, feeling a blaze of fire rush right past me.

Two things happened right then, one very good and one very bad. Alex's arrow successfully hit the final ghast, defeating it. But at that same moment, I found my feet on shaky ground.

I looked back behind me and saw I was on the very edge of the cliff, teetering, my feet half-standing on solid rock and half-standing on nothing.

I began windmilling my arms like crazy, trying to catch my balance and pull myself forward. I even dropped my sword to the side so I had both hands free. But it wasn't working. I was slipping backward! I saw Ossie running toward me, crying out, but she was a little cat and couldn't help me. Alex was dashing my way too, her hand stretched out, calling, "Grab my hand!"

I reached for her hand. Too late! Alex's hand was only inches away from mine when I felt my balance tip, and fell back, plunging over the cliff and into the lava below.

CHAPTER 14

WATCHED THE LIP OF THE CLIFF GO OUT FROM UN-
der me and saw Alex's panicked face as she hurtled
herself toward the edge, her hand still out trying to
catch me.

Everything was going in slow, terrifying motion.
First I felt my feet give out, then I was surrounded by
a rush of gravity as I plummeted. In those few seconds
I didn't look at the lava, but every inch of me knew
it was there. It was an ocean of orange-yellow liquid
fire below, ready to suck me in and never let me go.
No weapon, not even a diamond sword, was going to
protect me from that liquid fire.

I'm sorry, Dad, I thought as I fell. *I'm sorry, Maison.
I wasn't able to save you.*

It was all up to Alex now. Would she be able to find
the stones, build a new portal, and help Maison and
the others save the two worlds? Would she rescue my
dad in time?

I braced myself for the impact, my eyes squeezed shut. I pictured Dad, and Maison, and all the people I cared about, even that weirdo Yancy, and I said "good-bye" to them all in my head. Because that was the only "good-bye" I was ever going to be able to give.

But instead of hitting the lava below I felt something strong clamp around my hand.

My eyes flew open and I looked up. Alex was on her stomach, leaning half off the cliff, gripping my hand with all her might.

"Alex!" I said, relieved.

"Don't thank me yet," Alex said through gritted teeth. She was struggling to pull me up over the cliff. "Try to grab on to something!" Alex grunted as she strained to lift my weight.

My free hand reached out to the cliff and tried to catch something. I found my hands slipping against solid rock, not able to get a good grip. I swung my feet out, trying to plant them against the cliff. Nothing was working.

I felt Alex's grip on me start to loosen.

"You have to pull harder!" I cried. The longer this was going on, the more Alex's strength was being used up.

She reached down and grabbed my other hand. My legs kept trying helplessly to get some footing on the cliff.

For some stupid reason I looked down at the rippling lava. That was about the worst thing I could do. Sick with dizziness, I forced my gaze back up and shouted, "Hurry, Alex!"

"I'm doing the best I can!" Alex said.

I felt her grip on me loosen a little more. She was barely holding on.

I realized how panicked I sounded. I mean, I had a million and one reasons to be super panicked, but I knew that my panic couldn't be helping Alex, who had to be horrified enough herself right now.

"Alex," I said, "I know you can do this."

Alex's grip tightened on me.

"I've seen you take out mobs and face really scary things. And whenever something bad happens, you always find a way to fix it," I went on. "And you always like a good challenge, don't you? Then take this challenge and help me up!"

She gave one huge tug and pulled me back up onto the edge of the cliff. I was able to grab the cliff and hoist myself up. Solid ground had never felt better in my whole life.

For a moment I lay there on the red-black ground surrounded by fire. I tried to catch my breath, hardly believing that I was alive. Ossie happily danced around my head, purring and mewing loudly.

"Oh, man," Alex groaned. "Let's not do that again."

I sat up and put Ossie back on my shoulder. I picked up my diamond sword. "Alex," I breathed. "Thank you."

"Hmm?" Alex said. She was busy picking up her tools and toolkit that she had flung to the side to rescue me. "Oh, it was nothing." But I could tell from her posture she didn't think it was nothing. She had been scared, too.

Alex began quickly making another torch with a stick and piece of coal. We needed a new torch so we could find our way back, though I believe she also needed something to keep her occupied right then. I thought I saw her hands shaking.

When the new torch was made, she looked at the music disc with the glow in it. The glow had gotten stronger.

"Maybe the glow gets brighter the closer we get to the rocks we need?" Alex suggested.

"I hope so," I said, rubbing my aching back. My hands were definitely shaking. "I also hope we don't have to go over any more cliffs."

There was no way the Nether would be that easy on us. It turned out we did have to go over a couple more cliffs, and we half-inched, half-ran across them, wanting to be done with them as soon as possible. At the same time, we couldn't be so fast we'd get clumsy and have an accident.

We passed by more zombie pigmen and I kept my eye on them, but like Alex said, they left us alone because we left them alone.

Following the music disc's glow, we turned a corner and walked under a lava waterfall. I was a little nervous that sputters of lava might fly off and hit us. Plus I was nervous that mobs might be on the other side because the lava was blocking most of our view.

"It's glowing really brightly now," Alex said, studying the music disc.

When we stepped out from under the lava waterfall, a whole new section of the Nether revealed itself like a stage. We both froze, awestruck by what we found.

CHAPTER 15

IT WAS A NETHER FORTRESS.

I'd never seen a Nether fortress with my own eyes, though Dad had told me about them. Nether fortresses were like dark, enormous castles you could only find in this world. No one knew who built them, and inside you might find all sorts of useful things, like mushrooms, Nether wart, or even treasure chests.

But it was also a place where extra mobs, like blazes and wither skeletons, dwelled.

The Nether fortress in front of us was absolutely huge. All the people from my nearby village could live there and there'd still be room to spare! I wondered if all the Nether fortresses were this big and darkly majestic.

We could tell from the way the music disc was glowing that it wanted us to go inside.

Alex and I slipped into the Nether fortress slowly and quietly. Over to the right, we saw a dark hallway going as far as our eyes could see. The hallway had multiple doorways leading into who-knew-what. To the left, we saw the same thing—darkness and doors and more doors. It was so dark the inside of the castle felt as if it were made of shadows. We were thankful to have the glow from the music disc to help us see.

Without the music disc, we never would have known which one of those millions of doors to try. Thankfully, the music disc was helpfully pointing us to a very specific door.

"Watch your step and stay close," Alex warned. "We don't want any more accidents."

As if I needed reminding.

I heard a noise coming from the side and I swiped out into the darkness with my diamond sword. But I just hit the wall and knocked one of the blocks out of the way. Alex asked me to stop being so jumpy.

"Wait," I cried out. "I think there's something here." I knocked out a few more blocks with my diamond sword, then quickly drew back. At first it looked as if removing the blocks had given us more space, but now I saw there was no floor beneath them. If we walked over there without paying attention, we could have fallen through and landed . . . well, I didn't know exactly where we would land, and I didn't want to find out.

"Stop stalling, Stevie!" Alex hissed in a whisper.

This room led us into another long hallway. The more my eyes adjusted, the more I realized how red the walls were. Two doors were very close together, and the music disc wanted us to go through one.

A flash of yellow caught my eyes.

"Uh, Alex?" I said, hoping my eyes were fooling me.

"I said stop—"

When balls of flames came shooting out toward her, I lunged and pushed her out of the way. Almost immediately two more balls of fire blasted by our heads.

"It's a blaze!" Alex hollered, scrambling back to her feet.

The blaze came barreling out of the other doorway. Yellow blocks spun around a square golden head. Flames were licking along its body, as black smoke spiraled up out of its mouth. It was a half-mob, half-fire creature, and it had found us.

As we scrambled to our feet, we saw the walls around us burst into flames. Whirring wildly, the blaze shot more balls of fire at us, and all Alex and I could do was dodge frantically.

"Your arrows, Alex!" I shouted. There was no way I could get close enough to that blaze to take it out with my diamond sword. We needed a weapon that worked from a distance, but the blaze wasn't giving us enough time to do much.

Behind us, the walls of the fortress were engulfed in flames. Everything was fire and heat.

"Just run!" Alex yelled. We bolted through the doorway the music disc directed us to. When I glanced behind me, I saw the blaze slam into the doorway, shooting quick blasts of fire. The fire rapidly spread up the walls.

We ran and ran, passing several more rooms until we realized that the blaze had stopped following us.

"Oh, phew," Alex said. She looked at me very seriously right then. "You saved me. Thank you."

I shrugged. "I just reacted," I said. I didn't think pushing her out of the way had been as heroic as her saving me from falling off the cliff. But I guess either way we would have been equally doomed. I had just saved her, the way she had just saved me.

Alex shook her head and kept walking. "No, I should have known better," she said. "I was so caught up in the music disc I wasn't checking every corner."

"We all make mistakes," I said.

"Yeah, but every time I make a mistake, it feels like it gets rubbed in my face," Alex said. "You know I want to be an explorer when I grow up, but my mom's against it. She points it out every time I make a mistake as if that's proof I can't be an explorer."

Then her face hardened. Talking about our parents was mostly off-limits then. I couldn't stand to think of Dad in Herobrine's clutches, and Alex didn't even know where her mom was. She just knew that her mom had changed and turned against Alex after Herobrine started to gain power in the Overworld.

"Did you get close enough to the village to figure out what might be going on with your mom?" I asked tentatively.

"No," Alex said. "She's probably too busy being mayor of her own village to think about her daughter. And if she sees those wanted posters with my face on them, she's going to be especially mad."

That was true. But that was the least of our worries right then. We turned a dark corner and saw a magma cube in front of us. And as soon as it saw us, it jumped toward us in attack.

CHAPTER 16

AFTER GHASTS AND BLAZES, MAGMA CUBES DIDN'T look so bad. They kind of reminded me of the slimes in the Overworld. The magma cube in front of us was a dark red square with fiery red and yellow eyes. When it bounced, the pieces of its body separated, so it looked like it was made of different layers. Inside I could see it burning with lava and heat.

Alex and I had just come across a very, very dangerous mob.

"Watch out!" Alex cried.

I struck out with my sword, hitting the magma cube. This was probably the dumbest thing I could have done. Instead of defeating it, the magma cube broke off into several smaller magma cubes, and they all dove at us, surrounding us in seconds.

As they approached us, we had no choice but to hit them again with our weapons, which made the magma cubes multiply and multiply. First there was one magma cube, and then there were three, then five, then ten.

I continued to slash out my sword at them, to keep them at bay. If they landed on me, I would be badly hurt, and that would allow the rest of the magma cubes to pile on. My peripheral vision was full of red-and-yellow eyes and rebounding dark-red squares. I felt the heat of their lava bodies.

One magma cube almost hit Ossie, who was still perched on my shoulder. Ossie angrily batted it away. There were so many cubes I was hitting at rapid speed. One brushed against my shoulder and I cried out in pain. The heat seared me. I flung my sword back, slashing the magma cube that had hurt me, and then slashing out at the others. First they multiplied, and as Alex and I fought, they started to subtract. Ten magma cubes. Then five. Then two. After I took out the last one, Alex came over to check out my shoulder.

"Are you all right?" she asked, concerned and out of breath.

"Yeah," I winced. "It wasn't a direct hit, so I'll be okay."

Ossie got back up on my other shoulder. We moved in the darkness and turned another corner, coming into a deep, dark room that stretched out until I could barely see the shadowy end of it. The music disc began glowing like crazy, as if it was getting excited. I strained my eyes into the shadows. Could it really be?

Alex was thinking the same thing. We sprinted across the room, too scared to say what we were thinking because we didn't want to jinx it. But when we got to the other side of the room, the shadows fell back and we knew our eyes weren't tricking us.

"Oh, thank goodness!" I exclaimed.

Against the back of the room were piles and piles of the stones. The special stones we needed to build a new portal.

CHAPTER 17

EVEN THOUGH WE STILL HAD TO GET BACK OUT OF the Nether, I felt about a hundred pounds lift off my shoulders. "We found them, we found them!" Alex and I were chanting as we gathered up the stones. The music disc had led us to the right place!

It won't be much longer! I thought, as if Dad and Maison could hear me. *Hold on, because we're on our way!*

"Let's just get what we need for one portal," Alex said. "But let's come back another time and mine more so we can always have a supply handy."

I didn't say anything, since I didn't want to tell Alex I would be more than happy if I never stepped foot in the Nether again. Besides, we only needed that one portal, right?

When we stepped out of the room, bringing the stones with us, I noticed the music disc wasn't directing us back the way we came. It wanted us to go out a different way.

"Why do you think that is?" I asked.

Alex shrugged. "Maybe it wants to keep us from running into that blaze again, and the rooms it set on fire."

That made sense, until I thought about it a little longer. Why would the music disc protect us from the blaze this time, but not the first time through? It hadn't protected us from that magma cube, either. Or the ghasts. Or. . . .

"I don't think that music disc is trying to protect us," I said.

"Well, then maybe this way is faster," Alex replied. She was in a good mood from finding the stones, though I was already starting to worry about getting back to the Overworld. "Besides, maybe the music disc can't help having us run into mobs because there are so many mobs in the Nether. Maybe it's keeping us away from the worst mobs so we only see a few smaller mobs we can handle."

Soon we were on our way with the stones. The music disc led us through dark passageways and through gloomy rooms. I really missed sunlight.

"Look!" Alex said, pointing. "We're almost out!"

Sure enough, we were approaching a doorway that let us out of the Nether fortress. In the distance I could see the tiniest peek of the lava waterfall we'd walked under earlier.

Seeing the exit excited us and we sped up. We were super exhausted but the idea of getting out of this Nether fortress was so thrilling it felt like the equivalent of taking a Potion of Swiftness. I even forgot that my one shoulder still hurt.

Just as we were about to reach the exit, we were in for a surprise. Several dark figures stepped out, blocking us from getting through. In the shadows I could see they were tall, almost as tall as Endermen. In their hands they clutched black swords. They weren't moving very fast until they saw us, and then they came rushing our way like a small army, lifting their weapons to attack.

CHAPTER 18

"**W**ITHER SKELETONS!" I CRIED.

Skeletons in the Overworld were bad enough, but these wither skeletons were even bigger in size and their swords looked brutal! There was no way we could just run past them the way we'd managed to run past the blaze.

Alex drew back her bow and let an arrow loose, nailing one of the wither skeletons. The wither skeleton jolted, turned red, and then disappeared. Several wither skeletons came at me and I stabbed at them with my sword. Ossie got jostled on my shoulder and jumped down.

"Don't let them hit you!" Alex said.

That was good advice for any hostile mob, but *especially* good advice for a wither skeleton. If they managed to hurt me, they had a withering effect, which meant I'd get weaker and weaker.

I saw a wither skeleton advancing on Ossie.

"No!" I shouted. I ducked under several wither skeleton swords, rushing to save Ossie. Ossie hissed and jumped back as I slammed my sword down on the wither skeleton that had been going after her.

"Stevie, duck!" Alex called.

I obeyed. Two wither skeletons had snuck up behind me while I was saving Ossie and they were about to pounce. As soon as I'd ducked, Alex hit one and then the other with her arrows.

"Thanks, Alex!" I said, leaping back up and swinging out with my sword, hitting several wither skeletons that were approaching me. I could hear Alex's arrows being flung from her bow, one after another, taking out the wither skeletons right and left. The closer ones I went after with my sword. One good slash with my diamond sword and the wither skeletons fell away, until finally Alex and I stood in a mobless room.

"You're not hurt, are you?" I asked. In the craziness of fighting I hadn't been able to watch after Alex. Now I could see that she was rubbing her arm. I felt sick at the idea a wither skeleton might have gotten her.

"Yeah, just fine," Alex said. "How about you?"

"Fine for now," I said, picking Ossie back up. "Hey, what's that?"

Sometimes mobs dropped things when you defeated them, and I saw one of the defeated wither skeletons had dropped a sword. I picked it up and gave it a quick once-over. It wasn't as nice as a diamond sword, but who was I to turn down a free weapon that might come in handy? Alex nodded her approval.

New sword in hand, I said, "Let's go!"

We raced out of the fortress, letting its dark majesty disappear behind us. Under the lava waterfall we went. Back to the cliff and over the rickety, unsteady bridge. A few ghasts were seen flying around in the background, crying their creepy baby cries, though none came toward us. The music disc led us back, plus we had Alex's torches set up to show us the way.

"There!" I said when I saw the portal out of the Nether.

"What did I tell you, Stevie?" Alex said with a delighted laugh. "It might have been scary while we were doing it, but now that we're going to be out of the Nether, it'll make a great story: 'Alex and Stevie's adventures in the Nether.' Ghasts, blazes, nearly falling off a cliff, a few wither skeletons, a few close calls for both of us. . . ."

She was rattling on and I barely listened. I was counting the steps till we reached that portal and got out. The portal was beckoning there, its middle pulsing with a deep purple color. Against all the blacks, reds, and oranges of the Nether, that purple stood out like something magical.

I was still counting my steps when I noticed that the ground lifted slightly, and instead of lifting my feet high enough, I was gawking at the portal. One foot hit against a rock, and I felt myself start to trip.

I tried to catch myself, and it was no good. I spilled face-first, with Ossie jumping off my shoulder so she wouldn't land so hard with me. The sword I'd gotten from the wither skeleton flew out of my hand.

I lifted my head just in time to see the sword flying through the air. Everything was going in slow motion again. The sword spun, glimmered, and hit one of the nearby zombie pigmen.

"Stevie, you—!" Alex began in an outrage.

We were seconds from getting out of the Nether and I'd had the stupidest, most unfortunate accident possible. I'd made the zombie pigmen mad. As soon as that sword knocked into that one zombie pigman, all the others lifted their golden swords and ran to attack us.

CHAPTER 19

ALEX YANKED ME TO MY FEET AND WE RACED for the portal, the zombie pigmen right behind us, brandishing their weapons as they grunted and squealed.

"I told you not to touch them!" Alex screamed above the noise.

"I didn't mean to!" I protested. "I tripped!"

With zombie pigmen running at us from all different angles, the portal suddenly seemed much farther away.

A zombie pigman stood in front of me with its golden sword held up high. I ducked and slashed with my sword. Alex ripped out two arrows and struck two more of the zombie pigmen.

"Just get to the portal!" Alex stressed. That was already my plan of action, but it wasn't a very good one, because zombie pigmen go through portals, too. I was slashing my sword like crazy as I ran, knocking aside zombie pigmen left and right, getting them before they could swarm all over me.

The reds and blacks of the Nether fell back as my vision turned green and pink from all the zombie pigmen. There were so many! My blue diamond sword kept on hitting against their golden swords and throwing them back. Alex was shooting them with her arrows as they charged her.

Ossie had the right idea. Because she was small and wasn't human, she darted past the attacking zombie pigmen and made her way to the portal. Instead of going through, she turned and mewed at us, as if begging us to hurry up.

"Alex, look out!" I warned.

As a zombie pigman charged at Alex from behind, she dodged out of the way and I leapt forward with my sword.

"Remind me to thank you later for that!" Alex yelled.

Behind us we could hear more squealing and grunting. When we dared to turn back, there had to have been at least a hundred zombie pigmen running at us from the depths of the Nether.

"Run, run, run!" Alex said. A golden sword skimmed over my square head and another sword would have tripped Alex if she didn't jump over it. As we approached the portal, Ossie was getting more worked up, mewling and arching her back.

"Out, Ossie!" I shouted.

Ossie obeyed, gracefully jumping through the portal. Alex and I were right behind her, but at the last moment, several zombie pigmen stepped out in front of the portal, blocking us. Alex and I screeched to a halt. There were zombie pigmen in front of us. There was an army of them behind us. They were coming at us from all angles. We were trapped.

"Look!" Alex cried.

Just overhead, the greatest and most terrifying mob of the Nether was rising up. A Wither!

It was enormous, even bigger than some buildings I've seen, moving like a dark storm cloud. At the top of it were three black skeleton heads. Sizzles of black smoke rose from its towering body as it flew directly over us, casting a darker shadow over the already gloomy landscape.

The Wither began spitting out blue skulls in all directions. Wherever the blue skulls hit, there was an enormous explosion, as if the ground had been smashed with TNT. One blue skull hurtled out into the zombie pigmen army, knocking them back. Another landed just a few feet away, destroying the ground where it landed. A zombie pigman nearby fell into the hole.

Alex raised her arrows to shoot it. "Get back!" she screamed.

We both fell back as a blue skull hit the space just before the Nether portal, blasting out the zombie pigmen that had been blocking us and leaving a big hole there.

"We're doomed!" I concluded.

"No, it's perfect!" Alex said. "Zombie pigmen can't jump!"

She was right! Alex and I had to jump out to get through the portal now, and this meant the zombie pigmen wouldn't be able to follow us out.

I thought this Wither was the worst of the worst, and now I saw it had saved us without even meaning to. This gave me courage. "Let's go!" I said, grabbing Alex's hand so we couldn't be separated in the fiery chaos.

Alex and I jumped through the portal at the same instant. Everything went purple. Then we tumbled out into the Overworld, landing on our bellies, silky green grass beneath us and a blue sky above us. No zombie pigmen. No fires. No Wither. Sunlight!

I heard Ossie hiss, and I didn't know what she could be upset about right now. It was time to celebrate! But when I raised my head, my eyes widened in horror.

We were surrounded by an army of armored guards, all of them holding their arrows and swords at the ready. Standing in the middle of the guards was a tall and regal woman with red hair, her face turned into a sneer.

"There they are!" she said to the guards. "Arrest them at once!"

"Mom, no!" Alex exclaimed.

CHAPTER 20

COULDN'T BELIEVE IT. STANDING THERE WAS ALEX'S mom, my Aunt Alexandra. She was the most respected mayor in the area, or at least she had been before Herobrine brainwashed her. Now her cold eyes looked at Alex and me as if we were criminals, not family. And the guards worked for her, so they obeyed her every word.

"I'm sorry to have to do this, Alex," Aunt Alexandra said.

"Mom?" Alex gasped, her face pale. "You were the one who ordered our arrests?"

Aunt Alexandra sniffed. "If you break the laws, you pay the price. You brought that feared being into our world. As the mayor, I have to do what's best."

"But that 'feared being' is just a boy from another world named Yancy," Alex protested. "And we were all working together to fight Herobrine!"

As soon as Alex said it, I knew it was useless. Like my dad, Aunt Alexandra couldn't hear the prophecies on the music discs, and she thought we were making up all the Herobrine stuff.

As I expected, Aunt Alexandra looked even angrier when she heard the name "Herobrine." "I'm tired of your lies," she snapped. "You all know that Herobrine is just an old ghost story, nothing more. Now, where is the feared being?"

"He's not here," I said. "He's back in his own world, so there's no reason to arrest us."

"He's supposed to be in the *dungeon*," Aunt Alexandra said. "And why should I believe you?"

"Because we're telling the truth!" I burst out. "Herobrine is in the other world, the world where Yancy and my friend Maison live. I tried to destroy the portal there to stop Herobrine, but he'd already gotten there, so Alex and I had to go to the Nether and get the stones for a new portal. We went into this big Nether fortress—"

"Now I know you're lying," Aunt Alexandra said. "Two eleven-year-olds could not survive a Nether fortress. It's too dangerous."

"We did!" I said. "And Alex saved me when I almost fell off a cliff."

"Stevie saved me when I didn't see a blaze come out to attack us," Alex said. "And we got out together, even though we saw a blaze and a magma cube and wither skeletons and hostile zombie pigmen and even a Wither at the end. We did it as a *team*, Mom. We need you to join our team because we have to make this new portal and stop Herobrine."

"I've heard enough," Aunt Alexandra said. "Arrest them."

The guards began to move in on us, and Alex and I pulled close, not knowing what to do. That's when I heard Maison's voice call, "Stevie! Stevie, can you hear me?"

CHAPTER 21

Aunt Alexandra drew back in shock. "That music disc!" she said. "It talks!"

My music disc was glowing and spinning as Maison called out again, "Stevie!"

"Maison," I cried in relief. "You're still there. I was so scared Herobrine had gotten you!"

"No," Maison said. "The music disc here just stopped letting us talk. The technology is going haywire out here. The computers are turning on and off and— What's that, Yancy? Yancy wants to talk to you."

Aunt Alexandra covered her mouth in shock, her face had gone very white. "What sorcery is this?"

"Stevie!" Yancy said, getting on. "Hey, have you guys been to the Nether yet? I wanted to remind you: don't mess with the zombie pigmen. I mean, I know we all get a laugh at how funny-looking they are, but they really do cause serious damage, and they can follow you out of the portal into the Overworld."

"Uh, Yancy," I said.

"Those blazes are annoying, too," he continued. "And those magma cubes, ugh, I hate how they break apart. But if you run into any wither skeletons, make sure you pick up anything they drop. Sometimes they even leave their own heads, which is pretty cool. I've got a whole collection. You can even use those heads to make a Wither, which is like the baddest kind of mob in the Nether, and one I'd never want to run into—"

"Yancy," I said, more strained now.

"What?" he said, finally realizing I was upset about something.

"We just got out of the Nether, and we got the stones," I said. "Now we're surrounded by guards who are going to arrest us for breaking you out of the dungeon."

"What!" Yancy said. "By whose orders?"

"My mom's," Alex said softly.

Aunt Alexandra marched over to us and snatched the music disc out of my hands. "You there," she said loudly. "Who are you? What kind of trick is this?"

"Uh, hey, who is this?" Yancy asked.

"You're speaking to Mayor Alexandra," she said stiffly. "I demand to know what's going on here."

"Oh, uh, hey," Yancy said, on the spot. "So, um, Ms. Mayor, I am what you people might call 'the feared being.'"

The guards gasped and raised their arrows and swords toward the music disc, as if they expected to attack it.

"You're not the feared being," Aunt Alexandra said dryly. "You're a music disc."

The guards lowered their swords and arrows, looking a little embarrassed.

"I'm talking *through* the music disc," Yancy said. "I'm in my world, and I have a music disc here that lets me talk to you guys."

Maison got on. "Please, Mayor Alexandra!" she said. "You have to listen to us. I'm Stevie's friend, and I was the human from the other world who helped him stop the zombie takeover in the Overworld."

Aunt Alexandra inhaled sharply. "I heard there was a strange-looking girl who helped Stevie."

"Yeah, that's me," Maison said, though I could tell from her voice she didn't like being called "strange-looking." "What's going on now is the biggest threat the Overworld—and my world—have ever faced. Yancy, the feared being, accidentally made Herobrine real. The reason you don't believe us is because Herobrine is making you not believe us. Think about it! Do you really think your daughter would lie to you?"

Aunt Alexandra's mouth trembled, though she tried to hide it. "Alex had said that a music disc was telling her a prophecy about the Overworld being destroyed, but I saw no evidence of this."

"That's because only the people involved in the prophecy can hear it," Maison said. "We're the ones who are supposed to defeat Herobrine, but we can't do it if we're in different worlds!"

"And I know what I did before was wrong," Yancy said, chiming in. "Stevie, can you hear me? Stevie, I don't take it personally that you thought I was going to be the traitor. You had every reason to believe it after what I did. But I want to own up to my responsibility and I will fight Herobrine till the end."

"There's something else you should know," Destiny suggested. I could tell from her hesitant voice it wasn't something she wanted me to know.

My heart pounded. *Dad?*

"Herobrine has sent us more messages," Destiny said. "It's him with . . . with. . . ."

I took a deep breath. She was trying to think of a way to say it, but her dragging it out was agonizing!

"Stevie, he showed us videos of your dad," Maison said, cutting to the chase. "So now we know for sure that Herobrine has him and isn't bluffing. The good news is that your dad doesn't look hurt or anything."

If that was the good news, what was the bad news?

"Remember when Herobrine was talking about making me second-in-command," Yancy said, "and I wouldn't have it because I'd changed? Well, he made your dad second-in-command instead. Your dad is totally under his spell now and he's going to help Herobrine take over our world."

I saw Aunt Alexandra's eyes widen. "What!" she roared. "No overgrown mob is going to hurt my brother!"

CHAPTER 22

"**T**HEN YOU BELIEVE US?" ALEX ASKED IN AMAZEMENT. Before Aunt Alexandra could answer, one of the guards said angrily, "Don't be fooled, Mayor Alexandra. These kids are full of tricks, but none of them have come up with any proof of what they're saying."

Aunt Alexandra hesitated, weighing these words.

"But Mom," Alex begged. "You noticed all the weird things going on. Do you really think we'd be able to destroy all the property that's been destroyed and take all the leaves off the trees in the Overworld?"

Aunt Alexandra weighed this as well.

"I think I know how we can fix this once and for all," I said, and everyone looked at me. I felt a rush of courage, knowing what we had to do. "Please, Aunt Alexandra, let us build the new portal. Then you can go through it with us and see the other world."

Maison, Yancy, and Destiny all chorused their agreements to this idea.

"That's ridiculous!" the guard said. "Portals can only take us to the Nether or the End. Everyone knows that!"

Aunt Alexandra raised her hand in a way that let us know she had made her decision. "Build me the portal," she declared. "I want to see for myself."

Alex and I cheered and whooped, then got to work. We put the stones together, then over the music disc Maison told us to use flint and steel in the middle, just like making a Nether portal. After we did what she said, the middle of the portal began to glow in alternating reds, blues, and greens.

"That's not a portal to the Nether or the End!" protested the guard who really didn't like us. I recognized him—he'd been one of the guards to arrest Yancy before, and he was the one who tried to lock us up at Alex's place, but we'd escaped and rescued Yancy. No wonder he had it in for us. "This looks like more of a trick to me," the guard went on.

Aunt Alexandra examined the portal all over. "Or maybe it's more evidence they're telling the truth," she said.

"You can't let them off like this," the guard continued heatedly. "You said it yourself: you can't give your daughter special treatment just because she's your daughter—"

Aunt Alexandra cut in, "I also can't let myself not look at all available evidence. As a mayor, I need to keep an open mind." She turned and looked ruefully at the guard. "And if there is a Herobrine and he has my brother, I can't stand idly by."

"It works just like any other portal!" Alex said, eager to show her. "Watch!"

She leapt through and didn't come out the other end. Did we make the portal totally right and she was at Maison's house now?

There was no time like the present to find out. I plunged in, and Ossie followed me. Everything turned red, blue, and green, and then I tumbled out of Maison's computer screen and onto her carpet, Ossie landing beside me.

Maison screamed when she saw me. Before I could stand, she'd jumped on me and threw her arms around me. "You're here! You're safe! I never thought I'd see you again!"

And before I could even fully comprehend what she was saying, Yancy and Destiny were jumping up and hugging me, too.

Alex was standing by Maison's bed and grinning. "The new portal worked!" she crowed.

"How hard was it getting the stones out of the Nether?" Yancy asked.

Alex gave a brisk wave of her hand. "Oh, it was easy," she said. I don't think she saw me glaring at her because my head was mostly shoved into Maison's shoulder.

We all turned our heads when Aunt Alexandra tumbled out of the computer screen and on to the floor. Aunt Alexandra took in her surroundings. She was shocked.

"Alex," she said. "You were telling the truth the whole time. There is another world!"

"Welcome to Earth, the land of three dimensions, social media, and selfies," Yancy said cheerfully. "What do you think of it so far?"

"It's ugly and overwhelming," Aunt Alexandra said, putting her hand to her forehead.

"Well, aren't you full of compliments?" Yancy teased her. Destiny elbowed him and gave him a quit-that look.

Maison went to stand in front of Aunt Alexandra and introduced herself.

"You're the one who helped save the Overworld," Aunt Alexandra said.

"Yes," Maison said. "And now we need you to help save our world from Herobrine."

"Did someone call my name?" Herobrine asked.

CHAPTER 23

EROBRINE'S IMAGE WAS ON THE COMPUTER screen, smirking at us with his blank-eyed creepiness. In the background I could see Dad standing at attention like a soldier, holding his diamond sword.

"Steve!" Aunt Alexandra exclaimed. She tried to reach into the computer screen and grab Herobrine, but her hand went through and Herobrine's image continued to be there, unhurt. Baffled that she couldn't touch him, Aunt Alexandra took her hand back. "Where are you?" she demanded.

"Oh, now, telling you that would ruin the surprises I have in store for you," Herobrine said. "So, I see you've finally wised up and listened to your daughter Alex. Unfortunately for you, it's too late now."

"Give me back my brother!" Aunt Alexandra shouted at him.

Herobrine chuckled. "Oh, I imagine you'll be seeing him soon enough, but it will be when we're all in battle and he'll be attacking you, his own family. He's on my side now."

"That's not possible," Aunt Alexandra said. "My brother is a good, noble man who always stands up for others."

"Everyone has fear and anger in them," Herobrine said, his eyes glowing eerily white. "Look at you, Mayor Alexandra. You've never lost a single election since you've been mayor. There haven't been any mob attacks in your village since you came into power, and everyone around knows you as a beloved village leader. So why do you stay up at night, thinking about your failures? As a little girl, you dreamed of saving the world. Now you help end squabbles over chickens getting loose. Is that why you knock your daughter's dreams for being an explorer? Hmm?"

When I saw Aunt Alexandra's face, it had gone as white as Herobrine's eyes and she was sweating.

"Ooh, I hit it on the head, didn't I?" Herobrine said. "You're just a minor mayor of a little backwater village. You've never accomplished anything all that impressive in life, and it tortures you. You try to groom your daughter into being mayor someday, but it's all so that you can feel some sense of accomplishment."

Herobrine leaned forward. "I can look inside and see the worst of you," he said.

"Mom," Alex whispered, staring at her mother. "Is that . . . true? Do you really feel that way?"

"I. . . ." Aunt Alexandra said, unable to take her eyes off the computer screen.

"Some mayor," Herobrine went on. "You want to save the world, but you couldn't even save your own brother. Or your own world when your daughter kept telling you that I was coming to destroy it. You had all the warnings in the world and yet you did nothing."

"Don't listen to him!" Maison said. "He's just messing with your head, like how he messed with your head before to keep you from believing Alex. That's probably how he got Stevie's dad."

The mention of my dad brought Aunt Alexandra out of her daze. She slammed her hand fiercely against Maison's desk.

"I will bring together all the armies of the Overworld to fight against you!" she said.

Herobrine laughed in delight. "Wonderful!" he said. "I love battles! The more people hurt by them, the better. And you know this is leading up to the biggest battle any of the worlds has ever seen."

The earth began to shake!

Out the window, I could see all the leaves fall from the trees immediately. That was the sign Herobrine was coming.

"Earthquake!" Yancy yelled, grabbing on to one of the bedposts. I didn't know it was possible for the ground to shake like that. I fell on the floor.

"Ow!" I said.

Suddenly, the earth stopped shaking.

"My powers grow stronger," Herobrine said. "How did you enjoy that display?"

Yancy let go of the bedpost and walked to the computer. "You're a coward!" he said. "You fight from a distance and play cheap tricks like that."

"It's only what I learned from you," Herobrine said in a rumbly voice.

"Come out and fight us for real!" Yancy said.

"Oh, I will," Herobrine threatened. "I promise you, we will be seeing each other face-to-face very soon."

Even though he had no pupils, I could feel when his eyes zeroed in on me. "And when I do, I'll be sure to bring your father with me, Stevie," he said. "Just so I can watch him take you all out."

Aunt Alexandra tried again to grab him through the computer screen. Herobrine let out a delighted laugh and vanished. Even after he was gone, the terrible laugh still seemed to echo in my mind.

CHAPTER 24

AUNT ALEXANDRA PULLED HER HAND OUT OF the computer screen and looked down at it. "Alex, Stevie," she said, turning toward us. "I owe you both an apology. I should have believed you. And Alex, I shouldn't have let my insecurities cause me to try to make you the mayor someday. If you want to be an explorer, you should be an explorer. We can all do whatever we put our minds to and work hard toward, whether it's being an explorer or a mayor. And together, we're going to save the worlds."

She gave Alex a long hug.

"Yeah, family bonding can come later," Yancy said, not amused. "Right now we have a crisis on our hands. Do we have any ideas?"

"Yes," I said loudly.

Everyone turned and looked at me. I was even surprised by how certain my own voice sounded.

"Aunt Alexandra," I said. "We need you to go back to the Overworld and get the armies ready."

Aunt Alexandra nodded. "Yes, whatever you need," she said.

"And find out whatever you can about Herobrine," I said. "I know he's an old ghost story, but maybe there's an old story about him that can give us clues on how to fight him."

"Do you really think we can defeat him?" Destiny asked.

I looked around the room. At Maison, who had helped me defeat a zombie takeover. At Alex, who'd saved my life. At Aunt Alexandra, who was ready to move an army for us. At Destiny, who'd saved Maison and me in the past. And at Yancy, who didn't blame me for calling him the traitor even when it turned out I was the traitor and he could have rubbed that in my face. He was on our side now, I was sure of it.

"Yes," I said. "The prophecies made it sound as if it wouldn't be easy to defeat Herobrine, but they also made it clear that he *could* be defeated. And that if anyone could defeat him, it would be us!"

Ossie purred as if agreeing.

"I will go get the armies now," Aunt Alexandra said. "But how will you all defeat Herobrine?"

"The rest of us will stay in this world and find out everything we can about Herobrine and prepare," I said. "We're not going to let him have my dad, and we're not going to let him have this world."

"Wow, Stevie," Alex said, sounding impressed. "You didn't even sound this brave when it was about going to the Nether, and Herobrine is way more dangerous than the Nether."

I realized that, too. Maybe knowing I could survive the Nether gave me strength and confidence. Being here with my friends helped me, too. Sometimes you had to go with unpleasant options if no other ones were available, but sometimes life could also be really pleasant, like when it gave you friends to help you out.

"'Prepare?'" Yancy repeated, still stuck on that word I'd used. "What do you mean, 'prepare'?"

"Prepare for the final battle with Herobrine," I said. "You know there's no way he's being defeated without using all his powers first. He will create a huge battle with his own armies, and we will defeat him. Who's with me?"

I thought maybe the others would say all this was way too hard and they couldn't handle it. But they raised their hands and cheered their agreement.

Alex shot a big smile my way, hefting the quiver on her shoulder. "I always like a good challenge," she said.

To be continued. . . .

Check out the rest of the
Unofficial Overworld Adventure series
to find out what happens to Stevie, Alex, and their friends!

Escape from the
Overworld
DANICA DAVIDSON

Attack on the
Overwolrd
DANICA DAVIDSON

The Rise of
Herobrine
DANICA DAVIDSON

Down into the
Nether
DANICA DAVIDSON

The Armies of
Herobrine
DANICA DAVIDSON

Battle with the
Wither
DANICA DAVIDSON

Available wherever books are sold!

DO YOU LIKE FICTION FOR MINECRAFTERS?

Read the
Unofficial Minecrafters Academy series!

Zombie Invasion
WINTER MORGAN

Skeleton Battle
WINTER MORGAN

Battle in the
Overworld
WINTER MORGAN